I0586914

Also, By Luna Charles

Men Are Not The Problem
- Vol I & II

MAKTUB Trust Group

Presents

Men Are Not The Problem

VOL III

Luna Charles

To my sister, Magalie, who is always fighting by my side.

Table of Contents

Part 3

(ME, Myself, & I ...!)

We wish that we could change our past. What if we had a magical mechanism that could alter the space-time continuum? Somehow our lives would be much better. But what would you change?

If our mistakes created who we are, who would we be if we could change our past?

Steven Hawkins believed that for every action someone took, a different universe is created for the act they did not. Imagine endless worlds full of all your possible decisions, like if you had said no to the proposal instead of yes if you never had your child if you had that affair, billions of billions of parallel worlds of "ifs." But would you find the person you are in those parallel worlds happier than you are here and now? Would they be a more competent you? A more conscious person? Would changing who you were in the past make you a better you in the present?

I don't believe so.

I believe in life as well as in love. It is the trial and tribulations, as well as the victories we have, that make us who we are.

Shakespeare asked, "To be or not to be... Is it nobler to stand there and take the pain of your problems or face them with all you might in hopes of squelching the hurt?"

Fight, I say, fight because you secretly know you deserve a better life.

Fight because life deserves to be shared with someone who loves you as much as you love them.

Fight because sometimes, when there seems to be no end to life's chaos, just finding the will to fight will keep you alive.

- **Luna Charles**

Chapter XX

Just pay attention, and you will realize we're never alone...

I sat there writing for perhaps an hour. The words that described my past sorrows filled page after page as I sought to alleviate the burden on my heart by transferring the hurt to the folio. I knew my past as I knew the world. However, my love affair with José had been short by any standards and even younger by most. It had been confirmed.

At least, I hope it was as accurate as any love formed from the purity of interaction with no lust involved. Because in those days, I had not known my body's wants and could not seek out a relationship based on those wants alone.

Now I was beginning to see that it was a different story. And it made me sad to think that all those years following that first glimpse into what love might be, I had gone into relationships for the wrong reasons, chasing the wrong type of people and doing the wrong things. Then, finally, what I remember was the cause of Mrs. Jean-Baptist's death.

I closed the journal on my lap and took a deep breath. When I exhaled, there was no satisfaction in it. Instead, the exhalation was one of loss, regret, and self-loathing, three sensations that were becoming very familiar to me. It was beginning to dawn on me that perhaps after my relationship with José, emptiness, and pain had developed inside me.

Maybe because I had feared feeling that pain again, I had settled with just dating good-looking guys that did nothing for me except make me feel good about myself by being at their side, replacing real love for its egotistical version, lust. Living off the mental boost, the attendant gave me versus the high I would have lived on if it had been genuine love.

My mother, a hostile individual who believed in the power of negative reinforcement because that is how she had been raised, went out of her way to constantly batter me verbally regarding how bad I was and how I would never amount to anything. This resulted in me always wanting to prove I was better than everybody else and never being happy with being an average person that faded in a crowd.

That and the fact that she had always been too busy to give me the attention all children required while growing up, I was beginning to see, may have caused me to base my worth on the attention I received from others. And since I was a significant talent in any particular area, people would have admired me.

I resorted to getting it from peoples' reactions to the men I dated. José had been the only good thing in my life for a long time before Daniel; he never asked for anything from me and expected even less. So, it was a significant loss when I was forced to end our union for what I thought would be the best thing for him and his mother's relationship.

However, it seemed there was an underlying reason for my giving up José. Maybe, I pondered, I had let go of our relationship because I was not getting the outside attention I was used to having with —Sean—since dating the shy, quiet, and soft-spoken José.

The sun was bright, the sky was still blue, and I felt utterly alone. Sitting on the sofa, I stared at the sky, watching the birds fly by, my eyelids becoming heavy, my mind thinking of a Shakespearian play...

A Midsummer Night's Dream ... *"To sleep perchance to dream...."*

Borrowing words from a gentleman with an extraordinary perception of love, life, and reality in its many forms and lessons. My lids slowly lowered over coffee-colored irises. Then, breathing deeply, I fell asleep.

I walked against the water's edge, watching the tide overlapped sands, bringing crushed seashells and sliced seaweed onto my bare feet. The water was cooling. The temperature sent tiny shivers of pleasure up my spine each time it touched me physically. There was no moon, and it made no difference in the brilliance of the landscape, thanks to the stars.

I smiled at the heavens, feeling for no reason, particularly a sudden awareness of my minute place in the scheme of things, knowing without a doubt for the first time that I was never truly alone. At that exact moment, as God wanted to confirm my suspicions, an updraft in the wind caught my cloak and stole it away.

I turned in pursuit only to find my dress wrapped around my legs. Caught between clothing and wind, I was stuck performing an odd dance that could have been a cross between ballet and Flamenco, except with no music to accompany my movement. I laughed.

I did not see the stranger as he approached; I felt his presence, like his company, touch a chord deep inside me. The sound of his laughter joined mine and rang across the Pacific Ocean like chimes at play on the front porch of a small house in a hidden garden. The sound was beautiful and screamed of unknown and indecipherable mysteries.

"Are you so beautiful that Aeolus himself bid you to dance?" he asked.

With the asking of his question, the wind died. Leaving me facing him as if his attendance had been the source of the wind's life.

I saw nothing in his features. The light of the streets was behind him. But his height was prominent. Yet, his demeanor spoke of his gentleness as a person.

"I believe this belongs to you," he said, extending his arm to the side of him so I could see my cloak against the light.

I stood motionless, letting him come to me. Not even speech came to me from fear ... No, not from fear, it was an expectation as if it had been him that I *had come to meet. Closer he came, closer, and as he reached within six feet of me ...*

Ring, ring, ring.

It was my cell. Waking, I reached for the phone and almost dropped the glass of water next to it on the coffee table. The caller ID flashed Michael's number. I flipped it on before the next ring in the cycle had ended.

"Yes," I said, trying very hard to keep the feeling that had enveloped me while I had been in the dream.

"Where are you?" he asked.

"Where did you leave me?" I replied, a bit more perturbed than I had intended to sound.

"Look, I'm just checking on you, OK? I wanted to ensure you were OK and didn't need anything. Anyway, I'm across the hall at Jim's if you want to come over for a few."

I laughed. It was a bitter, cold, dead sound that came from nowhere.

"So, you did not even bother to walk over here after you came from the bar because you were so worried?" He said nothing, so I continued. "Did you get my prescription filled?"

"No," he answered, "They wouldn't let me. It is a prescribed narcotic. You have to show ID."

"Is the prescription with you?" I asked, not even bothering to ask why he had not just dropped off the prescription.

"Yes, right here."

"OK, I'll come over?"

We finished our conversation and hung up the phone. I lay there for a moment more, breathing deeply with my eyes closed, trying my hardest to recapture that feeling I had on the beach in my dream. The feeling that no matter what I thought and how I felt, I was never really alone. Instead, I found sadness buried deep within. Bitterness and insecurity from the relationship I had with Sean after José. Sean, who had been a good person, but a lousy boyfriend. His ways had left me feeling abused and unwanted.

I had believed somehow that I deserved the ill-treatment he had given and that I could not do better than him, so instead of walking away, I stayed. The lies got worse yearly, and I struggled to maintain the relationship. I assumed my resolve as a person was being damaged by the constant battle within myself was right and what was wrong. However, I denied myself the truth, instead turning to drugs and alcohol to dull my mind and senses.

Inside I knew I had a lot of anger that I carried within me left over from those days. Anger at the drugs I got involved with so that reality would not be so sharp. Anger at always making the wrong decision to please others instead of the right ones that would please me. Resentment for knowing what was right but doing what was wrong because, through the years, the fighter inside me had bowed down too many times, and now I was weak.

I should have stopped trying to please others the day I ended up in jail protecting Sean. I should have, but I didn't. So instead, I kept going with more drugs, lying to myself about my abuse. Pushing away friends that loved me more than I loved myself and letting myself crumble inside while I pretended nothing was wrong on the outside.

Exhale.

Not wanting to dwell anymore on the past. Knowing the feeling I was searching for was gone, at least for the moment. I got up and went next door.

Chapter XXI

The games we play...

As I walked in, the sweet, pungent scent of cannabis assaulted my nostrils. Ronny stood up. A shy smile lifted the corners of his face, making his greenish-brown eyes sparkle as he walked to the door to greet me. Michael remained seated on the corner of the blue sofa, watching the whole exchange between Ron and me while he puffed on the hydraulically grown chronic weed cigarette.

They all knew Ronny had a schoolboy crush on me, but I didn't take it as seriously as Mike. After all, Ronny was only eighteen, and though he rivaled Mike in size and looks, I had a little brother his age.

Kissing Ronny on the cheek, I walked past him and into the small living room. I greeted Jim and Bear, whose apartment this was. As I walked past the back of the sofa Jim and Mike sat on, Mike handed me the doctor's prescription. No one seemed to notice the exchange. Ronny had returned to his seat in the corner of the room. I joined him by sitting on the arm of the loveseat. Across the sofa, Bear sat on a recliner staring at me. I smiled to acknowledge his gaze. He nodded but kept staring.

"How was your nap?" Mike asked between inhalation of the joint in his hand.

"Restful."

He lifted one eyebrow, took another hit of the joint, and passed it to Jim.

Bear, whose real name I never learned, was close enough to notice the look on my face when I responded to Mike. A dark look passed over his too-pale-to-live-in south Florida features as he observed our exchange. Ronny saw it too. He gently elbowed me in the side to get my attention and asked me what was wrong.

He spoke so softly that I hardly heard him. I looked to my left, where Michael was sitting, and found him so engaged in the Grand Theft Auto, Vice City game he was playing that he wasn't paying Ronny or me any attention. I guess I had waited too long to answer Ron because he elbowed me again, a bit too hard this time. I flinched.

"Are you two OK?" he whispered

"Yes, we're fine, we broke up, and I'm looking for my place." I tried to sound very nonchalant about the whole situation but found my voice too melancholy to pull it off. However, when Ron started staring at me with more concern than I wanted from him, I forced myself to give him a small smile of reassurance.

"Why?" he asked.

"Differences in taste," I answered with what I hoped was an encouraging smile. "I can't live with an asshole, and Michael loves his stench."

Ronny began to laugh. It was not a quiet, controlled laugh. But a robust, hearty chuckle. That caused everybody to turn around and look in our direction. Seeing he had disturbed everyone, he tried to stop himself, which only caused saliva to go down the wrong pipe, resulting in his choking. Laughter being one of the best things to be contagious, I caught it and started giggling at Ronny's face turning red.

Looking very irritated, Michael asked, "What is so funny?"

Trying to ignore Ron, about to fall off the chair, I replied, "I was just telling Ron that my favorite part in "The Matrix" was when The Agent had Morpheus tied up and was telling him he had to get out of the matrix because the stench of men was getting to him."

Michael looked at me, annoyed, and Ronny finally fell off the loveseat. Bear, who had heard the whole exchange between Ron and me, only rolled his eyes and asked me if I wanted a beer as he walked over to Ronny to get to the kitchen. I couldn't answer him verbally, only shaking my head yes since I was laughing so hard.

"Hey, here, take this." Bear handed me the joint mid-stride.

It was halfway to my lips before a look from Michael reminded me that I couldn't afford to enjoy the intoxicating herb at risk of violating my probation because of my present legal circumstances. This is not to say I had not done much with Michael that would have broken my probation.

But because I was so close to getting off probation, he had constantly reminded me not to do anything because he didn't want to deal with anything that could hinder me from moving out and violating, and then being put on house arrest would definitely do that. So, I handed it to Ronny, who was now getting himself under control. Weed will do that for you.

Smoking the cigarette, trying not to choke, Ronny apologized for the problems Michael and I had as if it had something to do with him. I never understood people's reasoning for doing this. Somehow, they could have prevented whatever went wrong just because they knew the person it happened to.

Being the gracious person I was, I accepted, reminded him he had nothing to do with it, and asked if we could change the subject. Then, exhaling an almost clear breath, he opened his mouth to say something. At the same time, Bear called me to join him in the kitchenette. Ten feet away from the couch I was sharing with Ronny, it took me no time to reach his side.

"Here,"

He handed me a shot glass filled to the brim with dark brown, almost black liquor that smelled licorice slightly. In his right hand was the twin to what he gave me.

"He is a fool," he said as he stared at me.

I could not speak because his words had caused my throat to tighten for some reason or another. "And I promise you, he will regret it and soon." With that, he clinked his glass against mine and took the shot. I followed suit.

He handed me one of the three beers on the counter to the right of us and then walked around me with the other two. I stood there, letting the bittersweet taste of the German liquor run down my throat. Holding the glass so tight that the ink from the Jägermeister trademark on the surface of the glass was probably slowly poisoning my blood.

Was he the fool or I? *"Confucius says you fool me once; shame on you. You fool me twice; shame on me."* What about thrice? How big of a fool does that make me?'

I slowly loosened my grip on the glass and placed it on the counter next to my beer. The room had become strangely silent to me. Instead of the video games, laughter, and chatter of boys at play, my ears were filled with white noise, phantom sounds that could not possibly be part of this plane of existence. I grabbed the beer off the counter and downed half of it, drowning out whatever ghosts of my past had just threatened to reach me through the veil of time and memory.

My tear ducts filled and threatened to empty. I closed my eyes to prevent the escape of the salty water. Not here, not now, not ever. Blind to the world, in a self-imposed deaf state, I took another swallow of the beer.

Silently, Bear walked around me, opened the refrigerator door, pulled out the bottle, and poured two more shots. Blinking rapidly to clear my vision, I looked at him, six feet two, with dark brown eyes and hair. He was nowhere near handsome. However, he was not ugly. Bear handed me the glass again. And we repeated the ceremony from before, this time in silence.

He had already said what he thought was necessary, and I had been left dumbstruck. A tear escaped the imprisonment of my eyelid. He wiped it away.

The greatest thing a friend can be for another in a time of emotional turmoil. Is a silent witness to the pain and a Kleenex for the tears.

I finished the beer and walked out of the kitchenette, not bothering to kiss Ron or Mike bye, only pausing at the door to announce my departure. I left Bear and Jim's place and walked across the hall to Michael's apartment because it was no longer "ours," not that it ever had been ours, I supposed.

I walked through the door, and the dam I had constructed to keep my tears blocked shattered. I cried silently, deafly, and mutely, letting the tears that ran freely down my face be the only evidence of my pain. Cursing myself and my stupid sense of pride kept me here. Finally, I went to the couch and sat down.

I had to admit I missed my friends and needed them right now, and most, if not all, were only a phone call away. However, shame kept me from calling them and seeking desperately needed attention. The tears had lessened, only to be replaced by a dull, solid pain slowly spreading across my chest. I knew the pain; it was self-inflicted. It was caused by despair, loathing, and loneliness.

I needed something to dull the pain when everything else had failed me. I had always been able to find something to numb my hurt and disappointments. I couldn't smoke and knew nowhere to get anything else without Michael's aid. Nevertheless, I needed something. I hadn't always been like this, and I didn't consider myself an addict, at least not in the sense that I spent all my waking moments doing drugs or thinking about doing drugs.

No, it was just that I had given up dealing with problems without them. Dealing with everything intoxicated had become so much easier over the years. It had started with a couple of drinks to deal with my mom. Then, I had a couple of ways to deal with my stress. Then, it was a couple to deal with heartbreaks. Finally, alcohol became weed, the best, most relaxing thing to do when stressed. I loved weed, but I couldn't do it. It stayed in your system too long, and I was on probation, so I started with the Coke.

Michael had introduced me to the shimmery white powder. That and Ecstasy, Acid, Oxy, Zennies, etc., dealing with him had been a journey into a pharmaceutical wonderland. Each year, each new relationship and a new group of friends I had made because of my current boyfriend introduced me to a new drug I could use to numb the shitty way that guy ended up treating me. But with Michael, it was a never-ending experiment into how fucked up we could get and then have sex.

I remembered how the abuse had started. It had been part Sean, part pain, and part pride!

Forgetting the need for an anesthetic for the pain, I picked up my notebook from the top of the coffee table and started to write.

Chapter XXII

A tale of two Selene's...

"It was the best of times, the worst of times. It was the age of wisdom, it was the age of foolishness, it was the epoch of belief, it was the epoch of incredulity, it was the season of light, it was the season of Darkness, it was the spring of hope, it was the winter of despair, we had everything before us, we had nothing before us . . ."

When Charles Dickens wrote those words over a century ago in "A Tale of Two Cities," I was not born yet. However, no comments were ever as accurate in describing the year of my seventeenth birthday. So, following my friend's *instructions on how to mend a broken heart, I jumped back into the game. Within a month, I went through three boyfriends.*

None serious, none physical, and none I cared anything about. I was dead inside, never feeling anything from anyone. Like that night, so many months before Sean returned to my life.

Like a fog rolling in on a California coastal city, he slid down the block to hang out with Lenard and Lee, as he always did in the afternoons. I had almost stopped completely hanging out with them by then. Maybe it was my unfortunate fortune or a simple twist of fate. However, I was outside talking to them that day when he walked up behind me. I heard nothing, and they said nothing until his arms were already wrapped around me.

He pulled me into him, into an embrace of friendship, with the proposition of more. My body stiffened and then relaxed as I realized who it was. Lowering his lips to my ear, he apologized for his behavior from the years back that had cost us a relationship and for the news of my wrongly ended loved affair with José.

As he held me, I felt his heartbeat and the tightness of his muscles beneath the thin shirt he wore. My throat clenched, and my breath held. He was nothing like José. In fact, Sean was the opposite of José: Taller, rougher, a bit too rude, crude, and built from years of fighting for no reason. But there I stood, thoroughly enraptured from being in his arms.

Not wanting to, but realizing I had to, he could sense my rising desire. So, I stepped forward from him and looked up into his eyes' dark brown abyss, and at that moment, I was lost...

Happiness, sadness, friendship, hate, sex . . . it all somehow became one thing with him. I never knew how he felt, only how he made me feel. He was incredible in every way possible and devastating in all ways probable.

He lied to me, cheated on me, and never seemed 'there' when he was around. But the lovemaking was incredible, and when we were out, every girl stared at him like he was a potential meal. So yes, I would say that lust was the pillar of our relationship.

I tried to leave him and broke up with him countless times. I went out with friends and even went as far as dating Adrian, who is now one of my best friends and one of the reasons I'm still sane. But nothing stuck. Sean had a way with words, and he radiated this supernatural power. He always got me back. It was a cat and mouse game he played well with my heart.

I went from one job to another, somehow keeping a high GPA and managing to keep control of the walls that were my emotions from crumbling around me. While he hung out with friends, dropped out of school, and did whatever he did while I was not around.

In the third semester of my junior year, I found myself pregnant. There were no options; Sean didn't work. I wouldn't graduate high school for another year, and my mom couldn't know.

He borrowed money from Ken and took me to a clinic. Sarah met me there. The moment I woke up in the recovery room, he left. Sarah drove me home. I didn't see or hear from him again for two days.

It only takes a second of light for the truth to be revealed in the Darkness.

He apologized, saying he needed to think and I should have never had to go through that. He didn't deserve me. I was too good for him. So, I listened and said nothing, letting the ache that had been slowly growing inside me fester into something so acrid that each time I saw him, I would be so full of contempt that I had no choice but to hate him.

I asked him to leave. He did. I walked to Jeanne's house and said nothing vital to her except that I needed a drink and that Sean and I had broken up. She said nothing. She went to her brother's liquor cabinet and poured me an unhealthy shot of Jamaican over-proof rum. I took it in one long swallow and handed her the glass for another. All the while, I stared at her. Though I still considered her one of my best friends, I had always suspected that she and Sean had something going on, on the side.

Maybe it was how quickly they had become friends while he and I had dated, or it was simply my jealousy of her beauty and the fact that I always thought she was pretty no matter what. I only felt pretty when I was around my boyfriend; when I was not around him, I felt ugly and unlovable. Whatever it was, I wondered if he had been there with her in a more than just platonic friend sort of way the last two days.

Deciding that my jealousy and pain were getting the best of me and that Jeanne would never betray me, I downed the next shot without flinching.

Failing the fight to control my need for a narcotic remedy for my emotional pain, I closed the notebook and stood up, thinking about Jeanne and how I loved her. And how many times did guys that started out liking me end up with her? I had always forgiven her for it. Why had I always forgiven her, and why did I still consider her one of my best friends?

I did not know. Maybe it's because I always felt less pretty or more intelligent than her, and when somebody left me for her, I felt it was only suitable. After all, don't we all want the best out of life?

Feeling for the paper-written prescription in my pocket, I placed the notebook back on the glass table and headed toward the door. A little light-headed from all the drinks I had with Bear.

My front bumper scraping over the parking stopper/barrier while my front wheels suddenly stopped with so much force that it jolted me from my sitting position was my only indication that I had turned into the parking space in front of the pharmacy with too much speed.

Scared slightly from the sudden impact, I silently thanked God as I exited the car and entered the store in one piece.

The store was bright. The fluorescent lights that would have usually not bothered me were now penetrating deep past my irises and into my mind, causing me to wish for a pair of sunglasses or at least that I had drunk less in the last couple of hours.

I walked past aisle upon aisle of women's creams, lotions, diet products, and make-up toward the pharmacy in the back. No one was there dropping off anything except me, so the petite girl in the back of the corner quickly retrieved my prescription from me, looked up my information, and told me it would be ready in five to ten minutes if I wanted to wait.

"This is pretty strong stuff," she said. "If you don't finish it all, I'm sure you could probably sell it or something," she finished while winking.

"Yeah, well, I'll seriously have to consider that since I need the money," I replied

She laughed.

"Don't we all need the money right now?" With that, she walked away to get my medicine ready.

A few minutes later, I was on my way back to the apartment with a white paper bag in hand.

The pain came suddenly, a lightning bolt striking down upon the highest point on a barren plain and causing a ripple through the soil underneath. I was screaming, "Shut up," along with the lead singer of Linking Park, when the abruptness of the attack caused me to bite down so hard on my lower lip that I drew blood. It felt like someone was ripping out my internal organs with a rusty pair of needle nose pliers.

Stomping on the brakes to keep from causing a traffic accident, I miscalculated my traveling speed and slammed against the steering column, sending additional currents of pain through my body. I sat there, temporarily stunned by the impact. I could hear the squeals of tires from the cars that had traveled behind me as they quickly swerved to avoid a collision with the rear of my vehicle.

As the driver moved from my rear to my side. I heard the blaring of the horns and the curses mixed into them. Yet, I could not pay attention to them, too busy being doubled over against the steering wheel in pain. Tears ran down my face—face pressed against the steering column as I gripped the wheel with one hand and clinched the lower part of my abdomen with the other. I prayed to every deity in the universe to end the pain I was feeling, but now the pain was not just emotional. It was also physical.

Dizzily, I moved my hand from the wheel to the gearshift, sliding the car into park as I fought the Darkness creeping up in my vision, threatening to make me pass out. Slowly I moved, my head swaying from one side to the other. I reached across to the emergency lights on the dashboard, pressing the button with my index finger, hoping to warn any additional drivers not to get behind me.

I tried to steady my gaze, but another lightning bolt of pain rocked my body, causing me to cower against the seat. Finally, I gave up on trying to keep lucid and closed my eyes as I half bent in the fetal position against the car's driver seat. Tiny particles of light played inside my closed eyelids.

The world seemed to be fading to black, and I had given up all hope that I would survive this assault on my physical being. Instead, I contemplated how I would die alone in my car each time a shock wave went through me.

And when I thought the pain had reached its climax, when I was sure I could not endure anymore and would surely wholly lose consciousness, the pain stopped. There was no echo of it, no lingering reverberation. Instead, it was as if it had never existed, like the clearing of the clouds after a hurricane. It was like God, with all his infinite wisdom, had heard me and, for once today, decided that I deserved mercy.

It decreased with a rapidity that no medicine, no matter how strong, could have achieved. Sitting there for a minute, no longer leaning against the seat but up with my eyes open, I watched traffic flow moving around my car. Then, fearing that any wrong move would cause a reoccurrence of my previous episode, I gradually relaxed as I realized the worst was over. Finally, confident enough, I took the car out of its parked position and continued.

How little did I know of what was to come, or the confidence I felt at the diminished pain would be laced with apprehension.

Chapter XXIII

A drunk heart says what a sober mind can't...

I rolled from one side to the other, trying to get comfortable. The bed felt odd, and as much as I searched around for the sheet with my hand, I could not find it. I felt sick to my stomach. Nauseated from a night of too much drinking, a feeling I was familiar with, I lay there and tried not to move. I didn't want to run to the bathroom and hurl from the constant motion.

Instead, I wondered why it was so hot and where the breeze I felt was coming from. After all, Michael hated to open windows, and when I did, we always argued.

I opened my eyes as I lay flat on my back with my left knee bent. The sun hit me with full brilliance as its light penetrated the trees. The intensity of its rays spared no heat. It only took a few seconds to feel my face turn a pleasant 115 degrees Fahrenheit.

I closed my eyes again, thinking I somehow had a dream. However, the sweat forming on my forehead and running down my face said otherwise. Finally feeling uncomfortable, my eyelids lazily blinked open. I took in the early morning glow of the light of the lake as I lay on my back, thinking how queer it was for me to be awakening next to the lake!

The lake! What the hell am I doing next to the lake? I thought as I looked down and saw that I was lying on a dark blue plastic lounge chair. The shock and excitement were too much for my stomach to handle. I turned to my side, grabbed hold of the edge of the chair, and vomited. As my mind finally lost the last threads of sleep that had enveloped my thoughts, it was jolted out of any remaining haze left from last night's unknown adventures.

Sitting back up, I felt like a pin that had been hit by one too many bowling balls, and I quickly had to lay back down on the pool chair, which appeared to be where I had spent last night. Turning to my other side, I lay now facing the apartment complex's pool. No one was around in the early morning to enjoy the daylight or a refreshing dive into the pool. I was alone with my thoughts.

Each chasing the other like lost children on a search for their mother. A motion picture reel started unfolding with last night's event in my mind. The swift, painful episode on my way home from Walgreens, running into my neighbor on my way upstairs from the parking lot. Then, the Army staff sergeant, my neighbor Steve and I had drinks on the stairs after I had swallowed a couple of the pain pills, and we talked about my break-up.

I remembered the first shot of tequila and beer, the second shot, the third, the fourth ... then nothing. My mind was blank. I had blacked out. This was not the first time I had drunk myself into unconsciousness, nor had I awakened in a place I couldn't identify. However, it was the first time I had found myself outside an enclosed shelter.

Slowly, I tested my stability, lifting myself up to a sitting position. Then, feeling as if I was less likely to fall back down, I got up and began my trek to the apartment, hoping for no more surprises in my immediate future.

I reached the front door. The key chain with the little round piece of blown glass that Michael had bought me from the Amstel store in Key West during our first vacation and my jacket and cell were all waiting for me on the welcome mat. I paused for a minute. I still could not recollect all of what had occurred the night before. I bent down and retrieved my things, slightly lopsided as I came up. I stumbled into the door. I regained my balance a second before Michael opened the door. He looked at me like a stranger who did not belong.

He stood there, barring my entrance into the room.

"Are you calm now, or should I call the police? I'm not dealing with a repeat of last night. That shit was not called for."

I looked at him from a shaky perspective, hoping he could see on my face that I had no idea what he was talking about.

"Where did you go after that scene? I was pissed off but worried sick when I saw your car in the parking lot but couldn't find you anywhere."

"I apparently slept by the pool," I finally responded as I nudged past him and into the inner room. He was trying to deny me from entering.

"So, you didn't look for me that hard."

I sat down on the couch as he locked the door behind me. I felt like whatever was in my stomach was dying to make a daylight appearance. I leaned back and closed my eyes.

"I hope you know you're paying for the hole in the wall. But I do not have it taken out of my security deposit just because you got drunk, lost your temper, and tried to beat me!"

I measured three deep breaths, inhale... hold ... exhale, lifting my head from its reclined position on the back of the couch. I looked up at Mike.

"I'm sorry for whatever it is I did, but the truth is ..."

Inhale . . . exhale.

"I don't remember anything, at least not what you are talking about," I said as I glared at him.

He walked over to the wall that divided the small kitchenette from the living room and pointed at an indentation. It was hardly deeper than if someone had hit the spot moving furniture, but it had not been there before. I rolled my eyes at his obvious ploy to make the dent a bigger deal than it actually was.

"Well, let me remind you. You came home, and I wasn't here. You went to Jim's house, and I was there with the guys hanging and smoking. You made it a point to let me know that you were going downstairs with the Sarge and Steve to have drinks. I don't know what happened while you were with them or how many drinks you had. But I know the next time you return to Jim's place. You started an argument with me over what a selfish, self-absorbed asshole I am for doing this to your life." He stopped for a minute, catching his breath. I continued to watch him, knowing he was not done yet.

"You got into it with Jim. We left there and came here. You got worse and started screaming at me about how I'm just like the rest, and you were a fool to have ever believed that I was different. And when I make one small comment in my defense, you swing at me. Look at the wall. I would have had a black eye if I had reacted a second later.

How would I have looked to work with a black eye? So, what the hell is your problem? I can't deal with this. I said I would let you stay this weekend. But that's out of the question after last night's stunt. I want you out!"

He finished and stormed out of the room and the apartment, slamming the door behind him. I simply lay back on the couch and closed my eyes, secretly wishing I had at least given him a blackeye after all he had put me through.

He didn't mean what he had just said, did he? Deep within myself, I slowly withered, though I could not remember doing any of what Michael had just accused me of. I knew it was mostly true, given my experiences with alcohol and pent-up emotions, though I doubt that whatever had triggered me to throw that punch had been a *small comment*. Daniel used to always say, 'A drunk heart says what a sober mind can't.' For me, those words always rang true.

Alcohol, men, and my emotions, in that order, I never had control over any of them, and when all three were combined, it was a volatile cocktail. My love of life and beautiful smile were a cover for the terror-stricken mind underneath. And it was that terror, that fear of not knowing who I was when I was not somebody's girlfriend, which kept me repeating the same mistakes almost constantly in relationships. That fright forced me into relationship after relationship without the needed time for healing in between.

I sat on the couch for a few more minutes, letting my mind wander from the good to the bad and then to the worse. I was smart enough to know I deserved better and better sufficient to understand that Mike was not good enough. Yet, when you are too scared to be alone, you usually settle for less than your worth. He was excellent in the first month of our relationship, with romantic dinners, presents, and flowers. Then three months into it, Michael borrowed my car and forgot to pick me up from work.

He went out with his friends drinking and did not come home until six o'clock in the morning. That should have been my first clue, but I forgave him when he started crying. After that, things returned to normal: Sex, drugs, and alcohol. I thought we were good. Then, two months later, he went on an extended vacation out of town because he felt smothered.

I stayed there and let these thoughts run through my mind. This had to change, I thought. I'm not hurting anyone except myself. Then, as if triggered, a shock wave of pain swept through my body so intensely that I rolled off the couch and fell onto the ground. All the while trying to suppress a scream.

Curled in the fetal position on the floor, I pressed down where I thought the pain was originating, hoping the pressure would help lessen the distress.

It did not help. Clenching my jaw, I stood using the couch as a lever. Half-walking, half-stumbling, I reached the counter where my pain pills were. The bottle said one every three hours or as necessary for pain. I took two out, went for a cup of water that had sat on the counter since probably yesterday, and swallowed them in one gulp.

It was Saturday, and I felt like I was dying, hung over, and in pain. Hungry, I wobbled into the bedroom and fell on the bed. Reaching the drawer next to the headstand, I removed the four other pills to be inserted into me. I looked at the plunger and the pills as I followed the instructions on the box. Within minutes, I was asleep. No dreams came to me, and no angels visited me. Instead, I slept a sleep only intense drugs could bring to someone in my condition.

Chapter XXIV

Someone must die for another to live...

The flat sheet's red, blue, and purple pinstripes could be seen through it. However, the ruby tint made it only lightly so. As far as I could make out in what seemed like a waking nightmare, all the white, which was the central part of the sheet, had been transformed to red. Not pink as was the expected color of white and red when mixed, but simply red. A crimson color of the vilest and feared kind, not that of a rose or a card given on the day of St. Valentine, but a scarlet born of harm.

I woke in a state of confusion. A searing abdominal pain had jolted me out of my drug-induced slumber. I awoke to find my lower half engulfed in a blood-soaked sheet. The pain was so intense I folded myself into a fetal position and lay there amidst the carnage. Biting down on my lower lip, a spasm went through me, and a scream escaped my lungs to fall on deaf walls. I was alone in my misery.

The first thought that went through me was to move. I could not lay there and run the risk that the blood would seep into the mattress, though I doubted it had not already. I could not afford to buy a new mattress before I moved out. Half-crawling, half-walking, I wrapped the soaked sheet around myself and dragged the sheets off the bed with me. I bent down to use the sheet to clean the blood dripping down my legs. I had to stop it from running to my feet and into the carpet.

As I stood back up with the bundle of soaked material in my arms, I felt a mass drop inside me. It was as if an organ had been displaced and fallen to rest in the pit of my stomach. I screamed again at the pain and almost lost consciousness from the agony. Falling backward into the doorway, I used the wall as a crutch to make my way to the toilet.

I knew whatever was moving through me would not stay inside too much longer. I felt my insides open in an unwanted, searing, tearing motion and sensed the mass of tissue running down my inner thighs and into my panties as soon as I reached the bathroom door. I hurried to the toilet. I had tried to be careful with the carpet. However, in my dash for the bathroom, the sheet left a bloody trail on the white tiles.

Pulling down my underwear, trying desperately not to look inside at what might lay there, and at the same time trying to be so attentive that nothing would fall to the floor and cause me to have to clean it later, I sat on the toilet. Fear of dropping whatever was on the floor got the better of me, and I looked down into my panties. It was a mass of beef-looking liver. Red tissue with purple, blue, and aqua veins enveloped it. I gagged and held my breath. My hands jerked reflectively to my mouth, and the mass slipped from my underwear into the water basin. The splash it made as it landed echoed in my ears.

I fought the spasm in my abdomen and tried to regain my composure. Sitting down on the bowl, not wanting to look at it any longer, I continued pulling the undergarment down and off myself, now soaking and dripping with my blood. I could hear the dripping of my life force out of me, flowing from my insides into the toilet bowl, taking with it the life of an unknown person and hopefully the stupidity that had been my past.

One hand holding the gory mess of my underwear, I pulled a mass of tissue paper from the side of the seat, wrapped the whole thing in it, and threw it in the trash. I sat on the toilet for a while, potentially bleeding to death, not caring, only staring at the mess on the white tiled floor and wondering about Michael's potential reaction to it all. Sometimes life moves faster than one can or cares to remember. Finally, the red streaks on the floor melted together, and then I passed out.

I woke up still sitting on the toilet, not knowing what time it was or how long I had sat there. The drip, drip, drip, sound of my blood leaking into the toilet was the only sound in the apartment, so I knew I was still alone. Dizzily, I looked around the room at the mess on the floor, thinking if I had the strength to clean it up.

Placing my arm against the sink next to the toilet, I lay my head to rest on it and started to cry. I was going through one of the most physically and emotionally distractive situations and was utterly alone. But what made me cry was more than the fact that I was alone. It was the fact that instead of being worried for my own safety and well-being, I was more concerned about the mess I had made. I was worried about Michael's reaction to that mess and that I would somehow disappoint him. How dumb was I?

Yet, I mustered all my strength, cleaned myself up, and bent down to gather up the dirty sheet as I started cleaning up.

Swoosh, swoosh, swoosh . . .

An hour later, I was sitting on the couch in the living room. I had taken enough pain medicine to numb but not make me throw up from an accidental overdose. The TV was off. Nonetheless, I stared at the screen and listened to the washer as it rinsed away what I hoped was the last mistake I would make like this and any evidence I had for Michael of my pain. Oh, what a fool I am, not caring that I might be potentially bleeding to death, but only worried about Michael's fucking reaction to all the blood. Thinking that I was neither the first woman nor the last to put a man's feelings in front of my well-being made me sick.

I was dying. At least some part of me was, and where was Michael? Where would the knight in shining armor care for me all weekend until I was better? That would be by my side, be a shoulder for me to lean on. Where was the asshole? I had foolishly thought I was in love with him.

It had always been this way with me, I knew. I just denied it until now. I loved it too much and hard, preferring to make the person I was with at the time happier than I was in the hopes that he would reciprocate my feelings. I would plan romantic dinners, buy him expensive clothes and jewelry, and care for him how I wanted to be treated. Living my life by the golden rule of treating others how I would like to be treated. Nevertheless, in love, I see that was in some ways wrong.

I could not control someone's reaction, so to have spent my whole romantic life hoping for reciprocity was self-sabotaging because when they didn't give me back what I put in, I felt wronged. However, the fact is they had not wronged me. They were only themselves.

Yes, they were selfish and very often jerks, but I had been the one that had stayed with them, most of the time chasing after them.

The fucking "Golden Rule" does

not work, at least not in love. In love, you had to treat yourself how you wanted others to.

Chapter XXV

The Secret...

That night Michael did not come home until about ten. By then, the cramps that had twisted my body into a pretzel had dissolved. Since the unborn fetus I had been slowly killing had come out with as much pain as it had been pleasurable to create it.

I was lying on the couch, arms bent underneath my head, staring at the empty heavens when he entered the door. Neither of us said a thing. Instead, we looked at each other as he continued to the bedroom without breaking a step. I turned back around on my folded arms and continued staring out the darkened skies outside the open window. He wasn't shit, I thought.

Why had I put myself through that for him? No, I had not done it for him. It had been for me. I had done it for me, for my own well-being. I would not have been able to raise a child on my own, and knowing Michael the way I know him now, I was sure he would not have been a happy participant in my child's life. So, yes, this decision was definitely for the best, I decided.

I lay there in the dark and pondered the irony of finding the answer to what ailed me and possibly saving myself through the death that had just occurred.

Men are not the problem, I mused. Nor are they the solution. They are wanted but not needed, and it's when we, as women, decide that the men in our lives are so crucial to our overall happiness that we give up everything for them. In that instance, we lose any potential for true happiness and love.

After all, no one can be happy in a relationship when only one person is getting their way, and what's worse is I expected each of them to know what to do. However, no man can read minds. So, Therefore, for me to have gone into relationship after relationship expecting the person I was with to know how I expected to be treated when I never said anything—never told them when they were doing something wrong, was stupid. How could I expect somebody to treat me a certain way when I did not know how I wanted to be treated?

It is human to see the faults in others before you recognize the weaknesses in yourself. Till now, I had not wanted to see that the only constant presence in all my relationships was me.

So, if I wanted a better relationship, I needed to be a better Selene by learning to make myself happy before I asked anybody else to make me happy.

I sat there knowing all this to be accurate but not having the strength to embrace logic or reason. I was exhausted and in pain. I just wanted it to end so I could move on. But I knew the pain was a necessary evil. A reminder of what I had done. I remained on the couch and imagined a world without needing confirmation from others. Where self-love was abundant and something we were born with instead of something we had to learn.

A world where being a single mom wasn't looked upon poorly, causing more and more young women to find themselves in the same predicament I was enduring. I pictured a world where the lack of support from Michael did not affect my life, and I wasn't chicken shit and had been brave enough to walk away still pregnant, glowing with the joy of knowing I was the creator of life, and that responsibility was enough for me to have the courage needed to face the world. But instead, I daydreamed of my unborn child's laughter, and tears began to run down my face.

Michael had a nephew he adored. A smile almost always on his face. He was caring, reliable, and trustworthy. I would have defended his character to my mother and God alike. I would have bet my life on the person I swore Michael was as early as three weeks ago. Yet, thinking these thoughts, I valued my life too little to have declared it on someone whose character I had only known through the euphoric effect of drugs.

From Sean to Daniel to Michael, I have loved them all alike. They were all my first loves in their own way, and I had secretly hoped each would be the last man who would ever be in my life. So, I spoiled them, fed them, clothed them, and then finally put them on pedestals so high that I was burnt by the sun when I tried to reach them. But now, the sunburns were peeling, leaving behind a glowing, perfect tan of revelation, understanding, and internal beauty.

I was poised, positioned, and prepared enough to use the pain that haunted my past, almost killed me in the present, and threatened to ruin my future. To make a living, I knew I deserved and was within my grasp. But, so far, the only demon that all the writing I had done had exposed? Was the ultimate enemy that I had to overcome for success, me.

Yes, I had picked one pretty boy after another, one more charming than the previous, each at the end a bigger asshole than the one before, and as it had been *my* choice to be with them all, I had to take responsibility for the final tragic outcome of my Shakespearean style romance to each.

After all, I had not been forced, coerced, or intoxicated when I had decided to be with them. No, that statement was not entirely true. I had been at least partially intoxicated during most of my relationships. I guess that's what it took for me to remain blind to the fact that the guys I was supposedly in love with were assholes.

Anyway, that was then. This is now. I had to accept that I could not hold my past responsible for the current position of my life. I smiled at the thought of me in my three-piece Anne Taylor suit, perfectly manicured nails, and coiffed hair. I smiled even more expansive, knowing it was not an unattainable daydream but a very possible reality. Whatever I could imagine for myself, I could make into a reality. All I had to do was believe in myself as much as I had in my exes.

"Have you seen my baby blue tie?" Michael said as he walked up from behind so quietly that he startled me out of my introspection.

It was the first thing he had said to me since he walked in. It was funny because the question was so ordinary that it almost made everything seem surreal, a brief moment. I stood up and felt my inside shift down with gravity. As I moved toward the bedroom, I silently prayed that an unseemly mess would not fall from me.

I slid into the room, paying careful attention to each shot of pain that ran up my body with each step. I had no intention of speaking to him. He was no longer in my 'line of sight.' Instead, I moved from the doorway to the dresser. Removed a cigarette from his pack and walked past him onto the patio outside the bedroom.

As I sat down, Michael approached me.

"You're ignoring me now?"

He continued dressing outside on the patio.

I took a drag off the square and regretted having lit the damned thing. Oh well, I thought, it should keep me busy enough to ignore and frustrate Mike.

"I'm not ignoring you," I blatantly lied as I blew some smoke toward him. "Did you want something?"

"Have you seen my baby blue tie?"

I looked at him for a while, took another drag of the putrid tobacco stick, and answered, "No, why would I have?"

If looks could kill, I would not have had to worry about my resolution to be more self-sustaining because I would be dead on the spot from the gaze he bestowed on me. But instead, Michael pivoted on his heels and slid the door shut. So fast into place that it reverberated through the glass for a second. I rolled my eyes and went back to the cigarette.

Michael's a masochistic asshole. An emotional leech who was only happy when he was draining the joy from others around him. or everyone's attention was on him. The minute I started not to care, it began to tilt his emotional state, and soon Michael would start second-guessing his past actions and himself. Next, he would be nice and ask about my well-being. We had done this dance before, except this time, I was not doing the back-and-forth chase of the tango with him anymore. This was my last dance. I was bowing out.

As if on cue from some unknown director of the cosmos, the door behind me slid open. I did not turn around. I knew what the next scene involved.

"I don't understand why we can't be civil with one another."

In my head, I was laughing. But I kept smoking and ignoring him.

He continued.

"Now that this is all behind us, there is no reason we have to dwell on it, do we?"

Finally, I got up and turned to face him. He looked at me with expectation in his eyes. What was he expecting? Forgiveness, a torrent of words explaining my feelings? What? I walked past him and into the apartment, no longer caring about his expectations.

I grabbed underwear and clothes from the dresser in the bedroom and headed for the bathroom. Michael stood there watching me the whole time, waiting for me to acknowledge his existence. I didn't.

In the bathroom, I undressed and walked into the shower, removing the tie from my hair. I let my braids fall into the water. Then, standing there wholly immersed in the water, I turned around and moved the dial on the hot water to as hot as possible without the consequence of possible first degrees of burn. Letting it thoroughly wash away the dirt from my body that was my previous life, wishing the scorching heat from the water would somehow cleanse me psychologically, too.

Fuck that train of thought. I did not want to be cleaned emotionally. Everything happens for a reason. What doesn't kill you will only make you stronger. Where there is a will, there is a way ... and all the other Gloria Gaynor-type "I Will Survive" mottos in the world.

The only thing left to do was to make my next move.

Holding the air into my lungs, I thought about The Seven Sins. The wrath I had felt toward Daniel for his infidelity had caused my friendship with Michael. Lust had taken me into Michael's arms with as much passion as any woman scorned. Vanity made us work for as long as we did. Each was captured by the other's good looks, each enthralled by the reaction of others when we walked into a room. But when it was all said and done. It had been my pride that kept me with him. Good old fashion senseless pride.

What is it about our pride that can make a minor gaffe into a significant extinction-level event?

My major downfall has always been pride, stubborn as the goat, the astrological sign I was born under. I have refused to admit when I have made a mistake. No more, I promised myself. I would not let pride control me. I would not let the stubbornness that influenced my life any longer be the crutch that I leaned against for support.

I realized I should have never stayed with someone if the only thing keeping us together was one of the cardinal sins. Women presume we're weaker than we actually are. We know how strong we can be, but knowing something and acknowledging it are two different things.

Life, love, and reality are not about knowing. Instead, it's about acknowledging. Acknowledging when you are wrong and accepting the actions that must be taken to remedy those wrongs. And JUST ACT!

I shut off the shower, reached around the curtain to grab a towel, and wrapped it around my hair before stepping out of the tub.

As I pushed the plastic curtain aside to step out, I saw Michael leaning against the open bathroom door staring at me.

What the fuck ... I thought.

"You're beautiful, intelligent, and wonderful. I'm so sorry about all this. You deserve much more than I'm ready to give you now. I just want both of us to be happy," Michael advised.

"No, Michael, you want to make *you* happy. But, in addition, in the end, you are right. This is the best thing for both of us. I was not ready for a child, and I am glad you talked me out of it, even if it was by your deceitful ways. You are conniving, self-centered, and egomaniacal and are only happy when you're making people miserable, and I'm sure the only reason we got together in the first place was that you enjoyed the game you played with Daniel's feelings and mine.

Well, karma is a bitch, Michael. Moreover, you will find somebody you love to hurt you equally one day, and I will not be around. I only hope when it happens, you let it stop there with you, and you don't turn around and hurt somebody else."

I wrapped the towel around my body and tried to walk past him through the bathroom door. He blocked me. I backed off and stood inches from his reach, daring him with my eyes to do something stupid.

"Selene, I love and will always love you. We are just not on the same path right now. One day, maybe, if you'll have me back."

"Ha, are you serious? What is wrong with you, Michael? Look, I hope/wish? You all the best, but I'm out of here."

I stepped a foot inside the bathroom and closed the door in his face. I could feel blood running down my leg. Yuck! After cleaning myself and equipping my body with the essentials to keep my insides intact, I stepped back out. He had not left yet. I could hear the TV on in the living room. Wasn't he supposed to be going? After all, why would he get dressed just a few minutes ago, bothering me about his baby blue tie?

I did not care. Michael was not my problem. I left him on the couch and headed for the bedroom. ACTION! I thought. I snatched my cell from the dresser and dialed my mother's number without thinking about what I would tell her.

Chapter XXVI

Actions Speak Louder…

The phone rang six times before anyone picked up. But that wasn't unusual. Nobody picked up the phone at my mom's house, not even if they were on it, because to my siblings, their conversation was more important than the incoming call, no matter what that call might be. Then, finally, just when I was going to hang up from salvation, one of my younger brothers picked up.

"What day do, big sis?"

"Nothing, just chilling'. Is mom around?"

"Yeah, sure."

I heard him scream for my mom to pick up the phone. The clicking sound from the receiver advised me that he had placed the headset down.

A few minutes later, she picked up the phone.

"Alo," she said in that familiar groggy voice.

"Hi, Mom. How are you?"

"I'm OK, you know ... my back and sugar, but God is taking care of me. How are you doing?"

I did not want to ask her for anything. I always felt I was not worthy of her giving me anything. I took a deep breath and proceeded to explain to my mother. I explained to her the situation, well half of .it.

"Mom, I know it's a lot to ask, but I need a place to stay. I can't stay here. This place is not good for me."

She took a deep breath. "Selene, you know I can't have you move back in here. If the Government knows you're here, they might cut off my check, and you will be going out all sorts of times, and I don't want your sister around that. You are a grown woman. You should learn to deal with your own problems. If you move somewhere with some guy, you must tell him what you expect. Women are not cheap. You are not free. Stop giving yourself to these boys that don't know how to pay for you."

She went on like this for what seemed like forever. I bit my teeth and took it since I had been the one that had initiated the conversation between her and me. Then, when I didn't think I could take anymore without losing the sensibility and strength I had just found in myself, I thanked her, told her I loved her, and hung up the phone.

I had expected that, but she was my mother, and I was still hurt by it. I pacified myself with the thought that I had not told her the complete truth. Therefore, she did not know the extent of my situation.

Pushing my mother out of my mind, determined not to stay here any longer, I sat there and stared at my phone, compelling it to tell whom I could call that would help me out in this situation. Each of my friends I knew would be more than happy to see me away from Michael. However, I did not want to deal with them in my present state.

Pushing down the scroll button, I moved past Gloria, Jeanne, and Laneika's names. I knew I could have called, but all of them would want to talk about it and have me express my emotions. When all I really wanted to do right now was disappear into a cocoon until I was ready to reemerge as a butterfly.

Finally, I came to Sarah's name. Sarah, my best friend who deserved so much a better friend than I had ever been to her. Sarah, who had adopted me as a sister in the 10th grade. While I was going through all my ups and downs with Sean. However, I had never been as attentive to her as she had been to me. I had no better female friend than her since my sophomore year in high school. In addition, she, like no one else, would simply leave me alone to deal with my shit without bothering me to talk about anything until I was ready.

I pushed the call button while the screen still had her name highlighted. She picked up on the second ring, probably just leaving a club meeting from Nova, the university she was attending for business administration.

"What's up, girl? How are you doing?" she said in her usual perky voice.

"I'm good. Do you have a minute to talk? I really need to speak to you right now," I professed through clenched teeth, trying to bite back the want of crying swelling in my throat.

"Of course, girlie, I always have time for you," she said.

"It's just I'm tired of this place and this boy ..."

I started telling her that I was leaving Michael, and before I could finish the words, she was asking where I wanted her to go her door keys because she had classes early the next day and she knew I could not move back in with my mom. I almost cried but did not.

That is what friends are for, and I knew I was fortunate to have a couple of friends like that. Those friends really do not care what is happening. They just want a chance to help in any way possible. Sometimes friends are better than family.

After all, the old saying states, 'You pick your friends and get stuck with your family.' So, although it may take some time to pick the right friends, when you finally do, do not ever let them go.

I said my thanks and hung up. There was a lot to do and not a lot of time, and if I could not escape this place today, I would do it bright and early tomorrow. So I went to the drawer, saw a summer dress, Mike's favorite, and put it on.

Yes, it was conniving, but I was sure in the history of men and women, I was not the first nor would I be the last woman to try intentionally to make a man regret that they are a dumb ass for hurting them.

Feeling fresh and clean, I entered the hall and opened the closet. He didn't move. Making sure I made as much noise as possible. I pulled my suitcase from the top shelf. It fell to the floor with a thud, barely missing my bare feet.

"What are you doing?" He was standing right next to me. This realization scared the shit out of me because I had not heard him as he approached.

"I'm removing my suitcase from the closet."

He sighed. "I can see that, for what?"

"I'm leaving." I turned around as I dragged the luggage behind me into the bedroom.

"Well, not tonight. It's too late to go anywhere."

I placed the bag on the bed and looked at the alarm clock on the end table—10:30 P.M. stared back at me. Damn, it was late.

"Fuck, I was so ready to leave."

I remained there for a second, contemplating that it would take me at least two hours to pack and that Sarah's place was about two hours away. That meant I would not reach her until two in the morning, and God only knew if I would not be attacked by an aftershock of pain during my drive.

That second began to stretch into seconds. I couldn't lose momentum. If I did, I might be stuck here. I exhaled and began to unzip the suitcase. Michael grabbed my hand.

"What are you doing? It's too late for you to leave."

"I'm not leaving, Michael. I'm just packing."

He let go, and I kept going. Finally, I entered our closet and went to my side of the walk-in. God, I thought. I have so much shit I have to move. I went to the side with my evening gowns.

They weren't those huge bellowed dresses but slick, light, flowing. Each served as a memory of some beautiful Christmas night or real nice dinner I was so excited about that I went shopping for the occasion. I took each with the utmost care and laid them down at the bottom of the valise.

As I went to lay the last one at the bottom of the valise, a silver silk Calvin Klein number I had bought for a company Christmas party three years ago, I realized how long ago it had been since I had bought any new dresses. I held it in my arms, contemplating what that meant. Why hadn't I had anything to be excited about for so long? I stood there staring at the dress, willing the answer it.

I had been living a life with a person who had no excitement. This had been a charade, a pretense of what should have been a real relationship. An actual relationship would have had experiences to look forward to. Instead, I was anxious to see the person I was with, eager to go out with them no matter where we were going or how many times I had seen them.

Relationships should be a give-and-take, not so one-sided that you give all you are to make the other person happy. All that did was destroy one person's self-worth in the end. Seeing this dress and realizing that this union had not given me anything to look forward to in such a long time only reiterated how this union had never been meant. Hurting even more now from the weight of the newly learned truth I had just placed on my shoulder, I sighed and put the dress into the bag.

I sat down next to the bed, head in hand, to mull over the rest of the knickknacks I still had to pick up around the house. I needed a big box or several smaller ones to get my possessions in order. I wondered if there was one from my move to Sarasota only a few months ago.

"Mike?"

I called out, expecting that he had returned to the living room sanctuary.

"I'm right here," he said from the doorway. Apparently, he had been positioned there watching me the whole time.

I asked him about the box. There were none here, he confirmed, but he would see if Bear or Jim had one. He turned around and walked out of my sight line without additional commentary. I waited until I heard the door close. Sitting there, I exhaled one massive breath. What the fuck am I doing packing at eleven o'clock at night? I thought.

"Wow! OK, I am OK," I told myself.

Everything will be OK. I just have to take baby steps. I would pack, sleep, and tomorrow I would leave. I can do this,

I told myself. It's time I step away and admit that he's not what I want or need. God, I thought I loved him. But I didn't, and I don't need him.

And I knew that the worst thing that could happen in a relationship is when people start thinking they *need* the person they are with; love is a want, not a need. We will not die without love. If anything, the absence of it will make you stronger. You might not be happy, but you will not die from a lack of it.

I looked at the clock on the nightstand. Michael had been gone for a while, and my eyes were getting heavy and dry. I kept rubbing my face and yawning. I had been through a lot, and before I knew it, I had started to fall asleep. Michael awakened me by moving the suitcase off the bed. I popped up like the cork out of a champagne bottle.

"What are you doing?" I inquired

"Giving you room to sleep'" he replied. "You can't sleep with this thing on the bed with you."

I yawned, rubbed my eyes, and began to get out of bed.

"Stay," he implored. "I'll sleep on the couch."

I looked across at him and yawned again. "I should really finish packing."

"Not tonight. You're physically and emotionally, and I'm sorry."

He sat down at the edge of the bed and buried his face in his hands. It was not until I heard the sobbing that I realized he was crying. I lay back down and listened to him for a while. Why in the hell was he crying?

Inhale … exhale … inhale … Exhale. Just remain calm and aloof.

"Why are you crying?" I finally asked.

He cried harder. Between sobs, he managed to say, "I really do love you, and I don't want to lose you, but somehow things got fucked up and scary real to me. I'm too young for all of this. However, for the same reason, I do not want to lose you. Don't go. Maybe you can get a place close by and ...."

"Stop, please, just stop. You're hurting my head, and I don't want to listen to you." I got up and started moving around him. He tried to grab me.

"Michael, what do you want? I'm sorry that you're no longer happy with the decision that you've made, but this; this *thing* between us is not love. It's not real, and it's not going to continue. You love me. You hate me. You want me, need me, can't stand me, and want nothing to do with me.

Stop. You were right the first time; we are not good for each other. We are better apart. This is hurting me, too, but being with you hurts a lot more. Let's just enjoy our last night together, eat, drink, and pretend that this between us doesn't hurt like hell!"

I shook myself free of him and walked out. I was agitated and trembling, and my emotions couldn't take any more yo-yo-ing. I wanted a line of blow, a drink, and another line ... I wanted to punch something and scream. I wanted a lot instantaneously.

But I finally settled for the Coke since it was the most accessible. I walked through the living room and straight across the hall to Bear. When he opened that door, the room was filled with the coppery, ionized smell that anyone who's ever done Coke knew. He stepped aside just enough to let me in.

"Hey, you, OK? Last night was somewhat wild. Mike said you hit him."

I was glad this was Bear and not Jim. I would not have been able to hold my anger if it had been Jim saying this to me. I did not know why but Jim just got on my nerve.

"I almost hit him. I was drunk off medication and emotionally fucked up last night. Now he is over there having some kind of regret-filled break. Bear, I can't do this." I looked across at him. "I need a line. I need to be numb until at least tomorrow when I leave."

He smiled at this; he knew I was not a coke person. I didn't like the way I felt about it. But he had always debated using it as an emotional buffer with me. So, I was sure he was happy I took some of his advice.

"I will be happy to oblige," he said, slightly bowing as I walked into the room.

Inside, as if frozen in time, the same people played the same game in their seats. The only difference was Michael was not there. As I walked by, I had the eeriest feeling of being stuck in a *Twilight Zone*-like time loop. The hairs on my neck stood up, and goosebumps rose on my arms. I shivered a little as I said hello while passing by them to follow Bear. He went from the door to the glass table in a small dining room in a drunken beeline.

There must have been at least six grams of reflective white powder in what looked like a sugar mountain on the right corner of the table. I was not surprised by the amount, this was how they partied, and though I doubt they always had the money for it, they always seemed to manage. I sat down, half-expecting Michael to come knocking at the door looking for me and half-knowing he would not show his face to his friends in his present state.

Bear sat before the small snow mountain and picked up a razor on the table. I sat down in the chair caddy cornered to his as he drew the razor blade across the small mountain of off-white powder in a few horizontal lines. Cutting five smaller sections from the central mass. My stomach lurched and twisted in anticipation of the chemical reaction that the cocaine would have on my system. My abdomen shrank and enlarged of its own control.

"This is some great stuff," he started. "Better than I've had in a long time. I'm glad you decided to come by. I thought I wouldn't get to say goodbye."

"I'm sorry about last night. I don't remember anything, but I know how I can get when drunk and emotional."

"It's cool. It has to be hard going through all that ..." Bear stopped for a minute to look at me. He stared a little too long and made me uncomfortable, so I turned to look around again.

"You got a dollar?" he asked. I did not hear him the first time because I was staring to my left at the group playing a video game that seemed frozen in time. Then, finally, he repeated, "You got a dollar on you?"

I tried to shake myself from the zone I was in. "Yeah ..." I fished a ten out of my pocket and gave it to him. I didn't have any singles.

"Is this OK?"

"Yeah, that will work."

He took the bill and began to roll it into a cylindrical shape until it resembled a straw. Bending down toward the table, he placed one end into the entrance of his nostril while shutting close the other nostril with one finger. One line up one nostril, switching the makeshift straw's position, and a second line went up the other. He took a deep breath, fought the gag reflex in his throat, and handed me the rolled bill.

I took it. Still, a little zoned out. Flashes of the past flickered on the back of my cornea like slides from a projector. Alcohol and drugs, I ran for one or all every time I got emotional. I felt great at first, loved life at first, and wanted more at first, but eventually, the sun had to rise, and whatever it was that I was trying to numb out of me when I started was still there.

I looked at the bill in my hand, up at Bear, and around the room. How old were these people? One did not have a driving license because of one too many DUIs. Another, a plastic surgeon's stepson blessed with everything at his disposal, trying to be a thug, pushing daddy's buttons.

"Hey? Your hit," Bear said.

"Huh, oh, thanks, babe. Can I ask you a question?

"Sure." He laughed. "What is it?"

"How old are you?"

He coughed a little, I guess caught off guard by the question.

"Where did that come from?" He looked at me, and I could tell the Coke was already hitting him.

"I don't know." And that was the truth; I didn't know where the question had come from.

"That's cool. I'm twenty-nine. I'll be thirty in two weeks. We going to have this huge party. I wish you were going to be here. Michael is an ass, you know. He doesn't know what he got. I can't remember the last time I had a girlfriend, much less one that looked like you. I had to hire some bitch to break into my bed when I bought it." He started talking faster now, rubbing his nose, and eyeing the straw in my hand.

He went on, but I zoned out again. Thirty, I thought. That's not old, but not young either, especially to still live this lifestyle every night. This wasn't me. This wasn't the lifestyle that I wanted for myself. I looked down at the table and the rolled-up bill in my hand and decided I did not need a line.

"Babe, I don't think I will be able to sleep if I do this, and I need my sleep to leave early in the morning." It was a bad lie, but the only one I could come up with now.

He looked at me for a while. A small smile curled his lips, and regret showed in his eyes.

"You're sure?" he asked one more time.

"I'm sure." I stood and slid the chair under the table in one fluid motion while handing him the straw.

He took a step forward and wrapped his arms around me. I was caught off guard. I stood there stunned and frozen. Around me, the coppery smell of Coke in the air, the noise of the video game a few feet away, and his warmth against me all filled my senses. I thought I might never see them again, but things must end for others to begin. I closed my eyes and returned the love I was given by someone who had been a stranger to me until a few months ago.

"Bye, babe. I will miss you," I said.

"Don't say that. I will see you again," Bear said.

I stepped away and walked out of the apartment across the hall from where Michael lived, never looking back.

Chapter XXVII

Saying goodbye to yesterday...

I walked into the Darkness. The only light provided to me was the flickering images coming from the mute television screen Michael was watching. He lay on the couch with no shirt and black sweatpants. The lighting from the screen made his skin look eerily pale and his beer bulge more obvious. We looked at each other from a distance of what seemed like eons but were less than twelve feet away.

How do you say goodbye to something that was never yours?

How do you stop loving someone you're not sure you ever loved? Looking at him now, I saw that his nose was too bent to be ruggedly good-looking, his lips were too thin, and nothing about him made him spectacular. He was an average man in a sea of middlemen.

In fact, his hair was receding. His ears were too much on the Vulcan side of humanity to be attractive. But, when it came down to hotness, there was no contest. Daniel won. Tall, mulatto, hazel eyes. Daniel, who had begged me to return, whom I knew I still loved, still never left my heart.

I had run into Michael's arms, stupidly trying to use old, bad advice to get over him when I should have taken time to figure out what I wanted. Michael had been a mistake, a bad one. But one that I would learn a lesson from that I would never forget. Yet, Daniel was not the answer either.

I knew somewhere between the white and black of this episode in my life laid the gray clouds that spoke the truth. However, what did those cumulus clouds say about the path I was destined to take. No rain in the near future, maybe. But the rest is uncertain. Still, isn't that life a course of uncertainty?

Like the French say,

'C'est La vie.'

Plus, if we were to know the outcome before following the journey, who would we be then, and what would we learn?

I certainly would not know my capacity to endure. Like any person sitting in front of a psychic's crystal ball, apprehensive by what they might learn but full of faith, I approached the scene like nothing in the scenario bothered me in the least bit.

"So, you feel better?" he asked with all the venom he could muster.

"Yeah," I responded, not giving in to temptation. "But not from what you think."

He sat up and tried to look at me through the Darkness with only the aid of the screen. I flipped on the nearby light with the switch next to the door.

"You don't look coked up."

"I'm not. Did you know Bear was twenty-nine?"

"Huh, no, I didn't. Damn, and they're still living like that," Michael said as he returned to his comfortable position.

"I see that you feel better," I said accusingly, seeing him no longer crying or looking distressed.

"Yeah," he replied nonchalantly. "You were right. I was overreacting."

He turned off the television and looked back at me.

"I love you and always will, you know. Sometimes I feel you're the only person in my life that loves me and understands me, and losing you is something I'm not ready for, but I know deep down inside we have to go our separate ways."

He sat up and put down the remote.

"You are incredible in many ways, but you must find yourself. I thought you knew that. However, I've concluded that you're too dependent on me when you don't need me."

I looked at him across that hall. Somehow, this seemed all too familiar. I laughed inside, thinking about what Daniel had said to me once about me asking him why he did not try to get along with his father.

"'You know what the definition of insanity is, babe?' he had asked.

"It's doing the same thing over and over and expecting different results, and that's what I would be if I tried to get along with my dad, insane . . ."

That's what Daniel had said, and that's what I would be if I didn't realize Michael was right. I was too dependent on him, and I could do better.

"You're right. I really don't need you." I turned around and locked the door behind me.

"Have you seen my journal?"

"Nah, I haven't,"

He answered as he returned to his position on the couch and turned on the idiot box.

"OK, thanks."

I flipped off the light and looked for my lost memoir through flickering, colorful bouts of light and Darkness. The place was small, the journal stood out, and it did not take long to find. The thing about writing most people do not understand is that doing it may help your mind as much as breathing helps your body.

Into the bedroom I went, taking the journal in my arms. First, I sat on the bed and scooted up to the headboard. Then, sitting with my back against the headboard and pen in hand, I propped up the book and proceeded to flip through the pages that I had thus far filled.

My past made up at least a good portion of it. It was all well written, taking into account minimal grammatical errors. However, it did not add up to more than one hundred and fifty pages.

That's it, just a hundred and fifty pages. It was weird to sit there and realize that the mountain of pain, anger, jealousy, hurt, greed, and aggravation that I had felt did not amount to much more once I had written it down, put weight and substance to it, than half a journal.

It was enlightening to have this new perspective.

I remembered after I had been arrested for the first time because of Sean's burglary attempt. The judge seeing that I was a semi-educated, black female who had never been in trouble before, gave me a chance and put me on probation since my involvement had not been apparent.

My charge: third-degree accessory after the fact. My relief had only been overshadowed by my family's disappointment and the regret in my uncle's eyes as he looked at me no longer with hope and optimism but with failure.

Those eyes had haunted me, and when I smoked, trying to kill the cells that contained the memory of those eyes. All I did was find myself in front of the judge again, this time sending me to jail for violating my probation with the use of marijuana, but only for thirty days. He hoped I would learn a lesson from being incarcerated and quit while I was ahead.

I learned something about failure in that cell for several weeks with slightly under a dozen women. Not to say those women themselves were failures. However, they conveyed that mindset to each other. Each person there thought their situation was different. That each blamed the outcome of their present position on their past. Or on something that had happened in their history, they all thought of themselves as failures.

They all believed that if it were not for that particular circumstance, not one of them would have ended up at this place in their lives. They blamed the lack of a father, a mother that was never there, a rape that occurred, miss-education, lack of opportunity, lack of funds, early pregnancy, or simply believed that being from a specific neighborhood meant they were doomed to be where they were.

They had let one obstacle in their lives determine the whole outcome, making excuses about why they never tried to do anything different with themselves, and though the women themselves were not failures, their attitudes were.

I stayed there for those hours that turned into days, weeks, and listening. My mom had faced all those things and more, but she never limited herself to what she could accomplish. She never settled and never gave up when she was cornered. If anything, my internal compass screamed that women did not fold up like this. In those days in that cell, I learned that some women did not know what they could do in life.

More than a year after I had walked out of that jail cell in Miami. I sat flipping through pages of script that spoke of my past, laughing at some parts and tearing up at others. My memoirs seemed like some tale that one of those women had recited about the reasons she faced fifteen to life. On that page was the rape. Another page was me running away from being married off. Yet another carried the miss-education on that page, the drugs and lack of a father and a mother.

I realized that night there that I had inadvertently used my failures as crutches and weight to keep myself down, much like those women in those cells had.

I had hidden behind these obstacles as the reasons I failed to be who I knew I could be. Letting my past be the motive for why I would never be able to get beyond the repetitive circle in which I kept finding myself. So, I kept moving through the book until I hit empty pages, flipped a couple more pages forward, and stopped.

That's the end, I thought, looking at the journal pages filled to the brim with my past. I will only look back at that when I need to remind myself that I am no longer that person. I vowed.

I started folding the pages systematically, with one end folded to meet the center of itself, the next page the opposite corner folded to meet the center of itself, and so on. When I finished, I closed the book for a while, letting the air between the pages out, trying to fold them firmer so that the journal would not have an accordion look.

I reopened the notebook to the empty pages. Taking a deep breath into my lungs, I paused. What could I write to fill the blank pages that inspire me instead of discouragement? I exhaled. I wrote,

The effort to live according to what I want to accomplish in life, the effort to say no to the next drink, that night out with my friends, to that cute guy's advances just because he's nice. Am I worth that effort?

If I can make an effort to go to the mall and buy my boyfriend something nice if I think the man I'm with is worth the extra hour of preparation to go out with. Then I should also believe, no, I should know that I'm worth the same effort, if not more.

In my mind, I know of this battle. One side says your actions are correct and you should keep going. The other side counters: you're wrong and will never fulfill your dreams if you keep going this route. Angel on one side, the devil on the other, the age-old battle. Yet I have moved forward.

Somehow, with the small hope that I will wake up someday and, through no effort of my own, become the enlightened person who does not drink too much and does not do self-destructive things. And that I have become so self-aware that I will walk away from it all, start anew, and be the successful, intelligent, strong woman my mom always said I would never be.

That is a dream.

I know I cannot dream of myself as a better person. I've read the books, heard the tapes, seen the late-night infomercials full of these brilliant "how to's," but still, I cannot do anything but suffer.

Putting the pen down, I sighed, thinking about what made the teacher so different from the student. Then, retrieving the journal, I flipped to the inside front cover. There I wrote a quote by W.J. Bryan. I did not know who he was or what he did; for all, I knew, he could have been a she. I just knew the words were valid:

'Destiny is not a matter of chance, it is a matter of choice, it is not a thing to be waited for, it is a thing to be achieved."

I dropped the book and jumped off the bed to see where my dictionary was. I read a lot and sometimes ran across a word or two. I had no idea what it meant, so I kept a little Oxford dictionary in the closet. I found the dictionary and started skimming through the A's, finally finding

Achieve.

I read the definition. Achieve: to reach or attain by effort. I snorted to keep from laughing. There was that word again,

"Effort."

What is effort? I thought. I flipped to the E's. Oxford said, *effort*- was a vigorous attempt to accomplish. I already knew what vigorous meant. It meant to do something with physical or intellectual strength and power. I started laughing; the laughing became uncontrollable, which led to crying. Then, holding the stupid dictionary like a talisman to my chest, I sat on the floor and cried quietly.

The only thing I did with effort, I thought, was pretend everything was OK—that I was OK, that I did not feel secretly trapped in my own body. In fact, I was a great achiever at self-denial. Maybe I should have been a politician. But, of course, that is not what I wanted. What I wanted was to be able to keep simple promises to myself.

People try so hard to be honest with others, but how different the world would be if we put the same amount of time and effort into being honest with ourselves. At that moment, a thought came into my mind, as if sent from God himself directly to me. Moreover, I realized that no matter how odd that thought might be or how unexpected it was, it had never been more accurate. So, I rushed to my notebook, flipped to a new page, and began to write:

I can have it all.

No man shall stand in my way— including me. Though the roads I will travel may be unstable, I can have it all. Every time I have a negative thought, it will be fleeting.

Because I will remember my mother being kidnapped in the middle of the night while she was five months pregnant and being almost beaten to death for her political views. That she (a word is missing) escaped to Mexico only to be caught there and sent back to Haiti to try again. This time through Puerto

Rico, until she made it to the United States in search of a better life. I can have it all.

Next time I start believing I have not succeeded in anything, I will remember the nights I spent hungry, the baskets my sister and I carried on our head to market with our grandmother to try to sell the few morsels of vegetation we had managed to grow in a land deprived of minerals, trying to make money for food.

And if we could not sell anything, we would not eat anything that night. Now I have credit cards, bank cards, savings, a car, and the ability to go to restaurants or stay home to eat. I can have any job I want and live where I want. I am endowed.

Every time I want to push myself down. I will remember all those who die of hunger each day. I will think of all those who are raped, bought and sold, and incarcerated each day. Those that run for their lives each and day beg to live. Those mutilated, displaced, and hidden out of fear each day.

I am what I want to be and believe I am, and the only person who can keep me from achieving what I want is me.

Not education, money, criminal history, heartache, or the past. If restrictions had been all-powerful, they would not be called conditions, which is just a fancy way of saying a wall put in your way to jump over.

We as a people are only limited by our expectations of ourselves. We know this to be true. Otherwise, if our accomplishments were determined by the limitations we were born into, then no one could accomplish anything without being born with a silver spoon in their mouth. Tyler Perry would have never *had the audacity to show the world how mad a black woman could get. Oprah would have never shared her past with women to make them stronger.*

Wyclef would have never created a voice to define a generation of Islanders that had been silenced by famine and turmoil for over a hundred years, and Rowling wouldn't have produced the magic to inspire millions of struggling writers and poor single mothers worldwide.

I am my worst enemy and best weapon, and as long as I remember, I can and will have it all as long as I want it bad enough.

Having ended my internal monologue, I folded the journal pages, closed them, and restarted the packing like the pages in my notebook that I had folded as a declaration of freeing myself from the past. I would depart from this place and this relationship as fast as I could with momentum and courage.

I crept silently into the living room, pulling a container of personals behind me. Michael was asleep, snoring slightly in the light of the television screen. He was a sound sleeper, and though I did not worry about waking him, I started to pack my car with all the stealth of a Navy-trained SEAL. An hour later, finally done; I sat on the bedroom floor away from the sleeping prince.

I was looking through my notebook, yet again, trying to find fitting parting words to leave him with, something I had previously written, lost time until this exact moment when I needed it. Seeing what I had searched for, I ripped the page and folded it into a neat little square. Removing the apartment key from the keychain.

I tucked it into the folds of the folded paper. I placed the small goodbye gift in the living room on the bar counter. He was rolled into a fetal position, blond hair tussled everywhere, shirtless, chest slowly rising and falling with each breath. I wanted to bend over and kiss him. However, I fought the urge, knowing I would be playing with fire.

I began to walk to the door, pulling the suitcase behind me. As I reached the entrance to step out, I heard Michael stir. Through the partly opened door, I looked back at him. He blinked for a minute and looked at me. He began to rise, but I shook my head no. It had to end this way. I would leave this place like I left Haiti almost two decades ago, with no goodbyes.

Only vanishing into the Darkness to reappear somewhere else, starting anew in search of a better life and a better me. I looked at him one last time, and he at me. A tear ran down his face onto the sofa. I turned and walked out the door of my past and bravely into an unknown but welcomed future.

Foreword

Left behind...

Thank you for leaving me ...
Deceiving me ...
Never believing that I was worth
your love,
It was not until you left that I
realized you were right
So, thank you.
Thank you for the tears I cried ...
The pain I felt ...
The nights alone that I will never
forget
For proving to me that I am
stronger than I gave myself credit for
I thank you.
The blind can see, the deaf can
hear, and dreams do come true

with or without you.
Therefore, for leaving me …
Mistreating me …
Deceiving me …
I thank you for proving I am
stronger without you.

-       Selene

About the author

Luna Charles, is a Haitian-American writer who has authored numerous books, articles, and essays. Besides being an accomplished author, Luna is also a dedicated student of Theology, Metaphysics, and Philosophy. As a mother of two lovely girls, Luna has spent most of her life in South Florida.

Follow Selene's story in –

My Life My Rules

VOLUME I

Luna Charles

www.ingramcontent.com/pod-product-compliance
Lightning Source LLC
Chambersburg PA
CBHW072146130726
47909CB00004BB/1243